SATURDAY

OGE MORA

L **B**

LITTLE, BROWN AND COMPANY
NEW YORK BOSTON

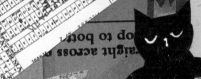

This morning Ava and her mother were all smiles.
It was SATURDAY!

Because Ava's mother worked
Sunday,
Monday,
Tuesday,
Wednesday,
Thursday,
and Friday,
Saturday was the day they cherished.

On **SATURDAYS** they zipped to the library for weekly storytime.

On **SATURDAYS** they lounged in salon chairs and got new hairdos.

On **SATURDAYS** they picnicked in the grass for a peaceful afternoon at the park.

And on *this* Saturday, they would also ride the bus across town for a one-night-only puppet show!

The day would be special.
The day would be splendid.
The day was SATURDAY!

Ava and her mother could hardly wait.

So—

ZOOOM!

—off they went.

But when they reached the library…

HELP DESK

Attention
Patrons—
Story time is
CANCELED today.

Please join us next
Saturday...

...storytime was canceled.

"Oh no!" Ava cried.

"It's canceled!" wailed Ava's mother.

They paused, closed their eyes,
and—*whew!*—let out a deep breath.

"Don't worry, Ava," her mother reassured her.
"Today will be special.
Today will be splendid.
Today is SATURDAY!"

So—

ZOOOOM!

—off they went.

But as they left the salon…

...their hairdos were ruined.

"Oh no!" Ava sobbed.

"Our dos!" boo-hooed Ava's mother.

H H!

pinza

They paused, closed their eyes,
and—*whew!*—let out a deep breath.

"Don't worry, Ava," her mother
reassured her.
"Today will be special.
Today will be splendid.
Today is SATURDAY!"

…was loud.

"Oh no!" Ava groaned.
"What did you say? It's too
noisy!" yelled her mother.

They paused, closed their eyes,
and—*whew!*—let out a deep breath.

"Don't worry Ava," her mother reassured her.
"Today will be special.
Today will be splendid...."

"TODAY WILL BE RUINED IF WE MISS THAT BUS!!!"

So—

ZOOOOOOM!

—to the *extra* special, one-night-only puppet show they went.

"We made it!" Ava exclaimed
as they arrived at the theater.

"Thank goodness!" Ava's mother
sighed in relief.

"Hooray for SATURDAY!"
they cheered.

THEATER

"Tickets!" chirped the lady at the door.

Ava's mother reached into her purse...

…but the tickets weren't there.

"OH NO!" Ava's mother gasped.
"I left our tickets on the table!"

As Ava watched, her mother crumpled.

"I've had it!" She sighed. "Storytime was canceled, our hair was ruined, the park was loud, and now we're missing the puppet show. I'm sorry, Ava. We looked forward to this all week, and I've messed up everything.…I ruined Saturday."

Ava was quiet for a moment.
Then she closed her eyes,
and—*whew!*—let out a deep breath.

"Don't worry, Mommy," Ava reassured her.
"Today *was* special.
Today *was* splendid.
Saturdays are wonderful…"

"...because I spend them with you."

So, slowly, hand in hand, off they went.

When they reached their apartment door, Ava turned to her mother. She had an idea.

"What if we…," Ava started.

"You know we could…," her mother began.

So they did.

What a beautiful day.

To my mom and to all of
the spectacular adventures
we've shared.

— OGE

ABOUT THIS BOOK

The collages for this book were created with acrylic paint, china markers, patterned paper, and old-book clippings. This book was edited by Andrea Spooner and designed by Sasha Illingworth. The production was supervised by Virginia Lawther, and the production editor was Jen Graham. The text was set in Adobe Caslon Semibold, and the display type was hand-lettered.

• Little, Brown and Company • Hachette Book Group • 1290 Avenue of the Americas, New York, NY 10104 • Visit us at LBYR.com • First Edition: October 2019 • Little, Brown and Company is a division of Hachette Book Group, Inc. • The Little, Brown name and logo are trademarks of Hachette Book Group, Inc. • The publisher is not responsible for websites (or their content) that are not owned by the publisher. • Library of Congress Cataloging-in-Publication Data • Names: Mora, Oge, author, illustrator. • Title: Saturday / Oge Mora. • Description: First edition. | New York ; Boston : Little, Brown and Company, 2019. | Summary: When all of their special Saturday plans go awry, Ava and her mother still find a way to appreciate one another and their time together. • Identifiers: LCCN 2018038326| ISBN 9780316431279 (hardcover) | ISBN 9780316527705 (library ebook edition) | ISBN 9780316431262 (ebook edition) • Subjects: | CYAC: Mothers and daughters—Fiction. | Adaptability (Psychology)—Fiction. • Classification: LCC PZ7.1.M6682 Sat 2019 | DDC [E]—dc23 • LC record available at https://lccn.loc.gov/2018038326 • ISBNs: 978-0-316-43127-9 (hardcover), 978-0-316-43126-2 (ebook), 978-0-316-52999-0 (ebook), 978-0-316-42123-2 (ebook) • PRINTED IN CHINA • APS • 10 9 8 7 6 5 4 3 2 1